PUFFIN BOOKS
AKBAR AND BIRBAL

Amita Vohra Sarin was born in Mumbai and grew up in New Delhi, where she obtained her master's degree from Delhi University. She currently teaches college courses in Indian art and architectural history in the Washington DC area, where she has lived for over thirty years.

Her first book for children, *India: An Ancient Land, A New Nation,* was published in USA in 1984. She has written widely on Indian history and culture.

Other titles in the series:

Akbar and Birbal

AMITA SARIN

PUFFIN BOOKS

An imprint of Penguin Random House

PUFFIN BOOKS

USA | Canada | UK | Ireland | Australia
New Zealand | India | South Africa | China

Puffin Books is part of the Penguin Random House group of companies
whose addresses can be found at global.penguinrandomhouse.com

Published by Penguin Random House India Pvt. Ltd
4th Floor, Capital Tower 1, MG Road,
Gurugram 122 002, Haryana, India

Penguin
Random House
India

First published in Puffin by Penguin Books India 2005

Copyright © Amit Sarin 2005

20 19 18 17 16 15 14

ISBN 9780143334941

Typeset in Bembo by Mantra Virtual Services, New Delhi

Printed at Repro India Limited

www.penguin.co.in

To my grandfather
Rai Sahib Shyam Das Vohra

Contents

Author's Note

In every era, individuals are born who try to solve the problems of their day with creativity and imagination. Akbar was one such person. At the age of thirteen, he became king of a country where he had lived only for a few months. He tried very hard to adapt himself to his new circumstances. His friendship with Birbal was but one example of his effort to learn more about his land and people.

Akbar lived at a time when travel was becoming easier because of the discovery of sea routes. People were encountering foreigners from other lands. Even in the sixteenth century, India had a diverse and multicultural population. Thinkers and philosophers were beginning to contemplate ways to unite different religions and creeds. Akbar was a product of his times. He was a flexible thinker who tried to experiment with new ideas. The issues that he was dealing with, however, are timeless.

Today, migrations from one part of the world are happening faster and faster. Many will live in countries that are different from the ones in which they were brought up. In order to adapt successfully to unfamiliar situations people need to treasure their traditions and yet, welcome new experiences and ways of doing things. For these reasons we should study people like Akbar.

Apart from Akbar's greatness as a king and person, in this book I hope to introduce children to the rich treasures of Mughal art and history. I am grateful to all the scholars, teachers and students who read through my manuscript when it was first written almost ten years ago, and for their support, comments and suggestions.

This work is based on serious research and existing folklore. I studied the translations of books written about Akbar in his time, as well as works of many scholars, researchers and translators in order to write this book, and regret that space does not permit me to acknowledge each source.

For those interested in reading more about Akbar and Birbal, there is a brief bibliography at the end of the book.

Amita Sarin

Introduction

AKBAR (1542-1605)

Emperor Akbar was one of India's greatest monarchs. During his reign of almost fifty years, he expanded his vast empire and built many impressive forts and palaces. Akbar was also a king who truly cared about his people and wanted to rule them with wisdom, understanding and religious tolerance. Though he was Muslim, and most of his subjects were Hindus, Akbar tried hard to ensure just and fair treatment to all his people, no matter what their race or religion.

Akbar's grandfather Babur was a descendant of the two fierce Central Asian conquerors, Timur and Genghis Khan. Babur established the Mughal empire in India in 1526 but died after ruling for only four years. His son, Humayun, became king but was soon chased out of India by his enemies.

During his retreat, Humayun married a young Persian noblewoman named Hamida Banu, who gave birth to Akbar in Umarkot on 15 October 1542. Astrologers cast several horoscopes for the royal infant, all foretelling that Akbar would be a great and noble king.

Humayun remained in exile for fifteen years and thus Akbar spent his childhood outside India, mainly in Afghanistan. When he was about twelve, Akbar accompanied his father on the expedition to recover his kingdom in India. With a small force of 3000 men, the Mughals defeated an army of 80,000 men.

Within a few months of returning to India, however, Humayun died in an accidental fall. The thirteen-year-old Akbar was proclaimed Emperor of India on 14 February 1556. For the next few years, his guardian Bairam Khan was the real ruler of the empire, but at the age of eighteen, Akbar dismissed him and took the leadership of the country into his own hands.

In every way, Akbar fulfilled his father's hopes and the predictions that were made about him at birth. Part of his greatness lay in his ability to pick the right men to do the right job. He was surrounded by a hand-picked circle of advisors, many of them Hindus. Although his nobles were proud and independent individuals from varied backgrounds, Akbar was able to unite them into a band of faithful followers. The most intelligent and competent people in the country—poets, scholars, philosophers, artists, musicians, generals and administrators—flocked to Akbar's court. In later times, some of these men came to be known as Akbar's 'nine gems' or *navratna*. One of the most renowned of these 'nine gems' was a Hindu courtier named Birbal.

BIRBAL (1528–1586)

Birbal's real name was Mahesh Das and he was born in Trivikrampur (near modern Kanpur). He came from a poor Brahmin family. He worked as a court poet and bard for other kings before joining Akbar's court. Because of his charming personality and brilliant wit, he soon rose to become Akbar's closest confidant and one of the most influential men in his life.

Initially, Birbal's main job was to compose poems and entertain the king and his court with tales and witty sayings. But later, since he could explain and negotiate in delicate matters, Akbar often sent him on diplomatic missions, especially to Hindu kings.

Birbal was also a brave soldier. He commanded an army of 2000 men and fought in several campaigns. He died fighting in a battle. But for the most part, Birbal remained by Akbar's side.

While Birbal helped his Muslim emperor learn about Hinduism, he himself tried to understand Islam and other faiths. In a world that was divided by differences, Akbar and Birbal were searching for similarities that would bring people together and help them to live in harmony.

The first time Birbal is mentioned in any of the accounts of Akbar's reign is when the king ordered that the mountain kingdom of Nagarkot be given to him as a *jagir* (landholding), in 1572. He must have been at the court several years, however, to have become important enough to have been given a *jagir*.

Around this time, he received the title Raja Birbar, which means 'best hero'. In ancient Hindu folklore, Birbar was a warrior so true to his king that he was willing to sacrifice his own life in order to save his master. Some scholars think that Akbar may have given Mahesh Das the title 'Birbar' in reference to this story. Today, that name is pronounced as Birbal.

Birbal stayed by Akbar's side for twenty-four years, which was half of Akbar's reign. Akbar visited Birbal's home on several occasions. This was a great honour. On two occasions, Akbar even saved Birbal's life.

When Birbal died, Akbar described him as 'the best among the best, the cream of our closest companions; unmatched, unequalled, unique in temperament . . . the very best among our loyal servers, the jewel of the king's innermost circle (of courtiers) . . .'

THE STORIES

During his lifetime, Birbal was known to have great influence over the emperor. After he died, Birbal became a legend and soon people began to tell anecdotes, jokes and stories about the friendship between the Muslim king and his wise Hindu 'minister'. Today, Akbar and Birbal stories are famous throughout India. Some tales may well be based on real incidents but it is difficult to be certain what the true facts were.

In India, there has been a long-standing tradition of stories about kings and their clever jesters or ministers. Often the same tales are told about different kings. In south India, stories very similar to those of Akbar and Birbal are told about a clever man named Tenali Raman and his king, Krishnadeva Raya, of Vijayanagar, and in Bengal about the clever court jester, Gopal Bhar. Such stories are also told elsewhere in the world, for instance, about the famous pair in Turkish folklore, Tamerlane and the Hodja.

All the stories portray Birbal as a clever and witty man with great presence of mind and a wonderful sense of humour. But Birbal is still a little-understood character. Many people think he was just a light-hearted jester and buffoon, while others see him as a hypocrite and flatterer. Some Muslims of his time blamed Birbal for taking the king away from his own religion, while others considered him a hero who advocated the cause of his people with the Muslim king. Birbal is also regarded as the champion of the oppressed because many stories show him as protecting the weak, the poor and victims of injustice.

HOW BIRBAL CAME TO

AKBAR'S COURT

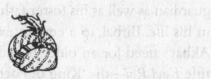

Nobody really knows when or why Birbal joined Akbar's court. Earlier, Birbal had worked as a court poet in the kingdom of Amber, near modern Jaipur, composing verses under the name of 'Brahma Kavi'. Before that, he had been employed by the Raja of Rewa (a kingdom in central India), a great patron of poetry and music. Some say that Birbal met Akbar accidentally and impressed the emperor with his ready wit. Others think that he was given as a present to Akbar by one of his former employers. Still others believe that the emperor demanded that the Raja of Rewa send Birbal to him.

A historian of Akbar's time mentions that Birbal joined Akbar at the beginning of his rule (1556) but he does not give an exact date. It is possible that they met when Akbar married the princess of Amber in 1562. The impressionable young man must have been fascinated by this charming and eloquent poet and storyteller. The fatherless king had just recently lost his guardian as well as his foster father, the two older men in his life. Birbal, to a certain extent, must have filled Akbar's need for an older friend. Akbar gave him the title *Kavi Rai*—the 'King of Poets'.

There are many folktales about the way Akbar and Birbal first met. At that time, Birbal would have been called by his real name—Mahesh Das. The tale retold here shows that Birbal was a boy when he met the emperor. In actual fact, Birbal was fourteen years older than Akbar. Even if they had met in the early years of Akbar's rule, when the king was twenty, Birbal would have been thirty-four years old. Still, as you will see, it makes for a good story!

A Meeting in the Forest

One day, Akbar went out hunting in a forest close to Agra, the capital of his kingdom. As always, the king was accompanied by a number of men, but as he liked to ride fast, he soon got separated from the rest of his followers. Only a few men were left with him.

Exhausted by the ride, the hunters suddenly realized that they had come so far that they were now completely lost. They had no idea how to get back to Agra. They rode on until they came to a place where three paths met. But there were no road signs, and they could not decide which path to take home.

As they were discussing the matter, a young village lad came along. He stared curiously at the richly dressed hunters on their horses. Akbar summoned the boy and asked, 'Can you tell us which road goes to Agra?'

With a twinkle in his eyes, the lad smiled. 'Huzoor,

how can this road go to Agra or anywhere else? Roads cannot move!'

The courtiers held their breath, shocked by the boy's impertinence. Surely the king would punish him for his rudeness. But the boy continued, 'People go from place to place. But roads cannot travel. Everyone knows that!'

Akbar was taken aback, and stared at the cheeky lad. Then he began to laugh. He always loved a good joke, even if it was at his own expense. He laughed until tears rolled down his cheeks.

'Very well, roads do not move. Can you at least find us some water to drink? We are very thirsty.'

The boy willingly took Akbar and his courtiers to a well and helped them get water to drink. Akbar was quite impressed by the quick-witted, bright young lad. He looked him up and down. 'Tell me your name,' he demanded.

'First tell me yours, then I'll tell you mine,' the boy replied.

Again, the courtiers were shocked by the village lad's impudence. One guard jumped up to box the boy's ears, but Akbar waved him away laughing.

'Well, I suppose it is only fair that I should introduce myself to you after all you have done for us. I am Akbar, the Emperor of Hindustan.'

The boy bowed low. 'I am Mahesh Das, Your Majesty. I am pleased to be of service to you.'

Mahesh Das showed Akbar and his men the way out of the forest and the road to Agra. Before he galloped off, the king turned to the lad. He had been very impressed by the boy's air of confidence. He was poor and shabbily dressed but he was not afraid to talk with boldness and humour to rich and important men. To the king, this was a sign of courage. People such as this boy were hard to find.

Akbar took off his emerald ring and presented it to the lad. 'We need bright young men like you in the imperial court. Come to my palace when you grow up. This ring will help you get an appointment with me.'

The Dishonest Gatekeeper

After his meeting with Akbar in the forest, Mahesh Das often looked at the emerald ring the king had given him. It was a big, handsome ring with a huge sparkling emerald in the centre. It was very impressive and, no doubt, very expensive. A man with such a ring would surely be very powerful.

Mahesh Das had spent his entire young life in the village but he was now ready to travel the world. He had heard many stories about the big city and the king's palace. It sounded like an exciting place to be in and he decided to pay the king a visit and see if he could get a job at the court. Putting his few clothes and the emerald ring in a bundle, Mahesh Das took off on the road to Agra.

For a simple village boy, this was truly an exciting adventure. There were many crowded bazaars along the route to the royal city. Merchants and traders from all over the empire sold their wares here. Mahesh Das had never seen some of the things that were being sold in the markets before.

He finally arrived at the king's fort and was quite awed by its magnificence. The massive walls towered over him. He had to tilt his head all the way back to see the very top.

Outside the entrance, a man was beating on a huge drum. He announced that the king was about to hold public court. Supposedly, any of the emperor's subjects could go in and see him, but access to the king wasn't quite that simple. Tall sentries with lances and swords stood barring the way. A crowd of people milled around them. Many had travelled far to bring their problem to the king's attention. Some people had pieces of paper on which their petitions were written. Others had letters from important men, advancing their causes. Still others were bribing the guards to allow them to enter.

Mahesh Das pushed his way through the crowd and went up to one of the gatekeepers. 'I have come to see the king. May I go in?' he asked politely.

The tall sentry looked down in amazement at the shabby, young village boy. What nerve, expecting to be let in without a gift for the guard, or even a letter of introduction! This young fellow was obviously entirely ignorant of the ways of the world. Anyway, he didn't look as though he had the money to offer a decent bribe. The guard began to ridicule him.

'Ah, so you've come to see the king, have you? Do you have a personal invitation from His Majesty to dine with him in his private dining chamber? Or perhaps you are so important that the emperor will leave everything he is doing to chat with you. Off with you, miserable scamp! The king doesn't have time for the likes of you.'

Mahesh Das was a bit intimidated but he held his ground. He remembered the emerald ring. Quickly he took it out of his bundle and showed it to the guard.

'The king gave me this ring some years ago. He said it would help me get an appointment with him.'

Stunned, the guard examined the ring. He showed it to the other guards. It appeared to be genuine.

The sentry stroked his moustache thoughtfully. Perhaps the young man was not as unimportant as he seemed. Perhaps he was not too poor either, and could afford to give the gatekeeper a gift. 'If I let you in, what will you give me? A cow, a cock, embroidered slippers, a silken gown ... Everyone gives me something.'

'At the moment, I have nothing with me,' said the boy, thinking quickly. 'But surely the king will give me a reward, and that I will gladly share with you—half mine, half yours.'

'You have to come back out this way. Mind you keep your word ... or else!' the greedy gatekeeper said threateningly. He let Mahesh Das in, brandishing his sword.

The grandeur of the Public Hall of Audience took the villager's breath away. The buildings were made of red sandstone and the floors were covered with beautiful carpets. More than a hundred richly carved pillars surrounded the courtyard where the common people stood to see the king. In an enclosed balcony, on a platform covered with rich silken fabrics, sat the emperor supported by bolster cushions. He was wearing simple but costly garments. The nobles around him wore magnificent brocades. Mahesh Das was quite awed by the splendour of the palace.

When the officer of the court signalled him to approach the king, Mahesh Das stumbled forward and bowed his head as he had seen the others do. Then he held out the emerald ring, and stood silently, unable to speak. Akbar had a keen memory and immediately recognized the ring and the boy who had helped him out of the forest.

He smiled kindly. 'So, Mahesh Das, you decided to pay me a visit after all! Tell me what would you like to have? I never rewarded you for your help in the forest.

You can name your gift.'

By this time, Mahesh Das had recovered his composure. He was still smarting from the treatment he had received at the hands of the greedy guard. He bowed again and said, 'The sight of Your Majesty is reward enough for me. But if you insist on giving me something as a token of your regard, then I would like to receive one hundred lashes on my bare back.'

Akbar and all his courtiers were astounded by this peculiar request. The boy looked poor. Akbar expected him to ask for gold or jewels but instead he asked to be beaten! This was most strange.

Akbar looked closely at the boy's face. He seemed to be suppressing a smile. This was a very intelligent young person. He was trying to tell the emperor something in his own way. He summoned the court soldier who stood by with his whip, waiting to punish whomever the emperor ordered.

'Mahesh Das, if this is what you really want, I will order my man to give you a hundred lashes on your bare back.'

The soldier lifted his whip and Mahesh Das removed his shirt, but before the soldier began his task, the lad help up his hand.

'First I must keep my promise to the sentry at the gate. I assured him that I would share whatever I received from the emperor with him—half mine, half his. Can he get his fifty lashes first?'

Akbar was furious. So this is what the corrupt guards did to the poor people who came to see their king! They demanded bribes and gifts. Akbar had the dishonest gatekeeper brought into the open court. When the man saw Mahesh Das, he realized that the boy had complained about him. He threw himself at Akbar's feet and begged for mercy. The emperor sternly ordered that all hundred lashes be given to the man as a lesson to him and to his fellow gatekeepers.

Akbar turned to Mahesh Das. He was very pleased at the way in which the clever young man had paid the dishonest gatekeeper back for his greediness. His actions confirmed what Akbar had thought at his first meeting—that Mahesh Das was an intelligent and quick-witted fellow. Even though he was poor, he had the courage to stand up to bullies and the wits to set them right.

He said to his visitor, 'I need people like you around me, Mahesh Das. Honest and brave men are difficult to find. Stay on at court and help me run my kingdom.'

And this was the beginning of a lifelong friendship between the two men.

THE PILLAR

OF

JUSTICE

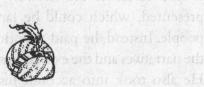

As the 'shadow of God on earth', it was the emperor's duty to establish peace and order in his kingdom by protecting the weak and punishing the wicked.

Akbar prided himself on his fairness. To his people he was 'Jahanpanah', The Refuge of the World. If he couldn't help his subjects with their problems, nobody could. Every day, Akbar and his advisors, including Birbal, sat in the Hall of Public Audience to hear people's grievances. They would spend several hours listening to reports, conducting the business of the empire and hearing cases brought before the court. A large drum would be beaten loudly to announce to the public that the king was holding court, and even common folk could then be admitted into Akbar's presence if they had any complaints or requests.

Akbar observed the accused carefully to see from his expression and behaviour if he was telling the truth. According to his biographer Abul Fazl, when Akbar judged cases, he did not rely only on the evidence presented, which could be tampered with by crafty people. Instead, he paid attention to contradictions in the narratives and the expressions of the people involved. He also took into account his own knowledge and experience.

In his judgements, the emperor was advised by the *ulama*, who were specialists in Muslim law. Strict laws were laid down to help the *qazis* (judges) in administering justice. Islamic law consisted of two parts—religious, which applied only to Muslims, and secular, for Muslims as well as non-Muslims. (Later in his reign, Akbar made a new rule that learned Brahmins, rather than Muslim *qazis*, should decide cases involving Hindus.) Decisions would be made in consultation with the law officers, scribes would take detailed notes and the clerks would draw up the orders. Then the judgements and orders would be sent to the proper official under the imperial seal.

In 1578, when Akbar visited Punjab, he found that the legal system there was in a mess. Afghan traders, who had recently settled in the towns and villages, seemed to be taking advantage of the helpless. Birbal was sent off with another nobleman to Punjab to inquire into the matter and to help the needy obtain land from the government.

As a result of this and other such experiences, Birbal became very concerned about the oppression of the poor. On 11 March 1582 at the New Year Festival, Birbal requested that trustworthy individuals be posted at the gates of the palace to make certain that anyone who had been wronged would be able to complain directly to the king.

In 1583, Akbar established a Department of Administration and appointed his most trusted nobles, including Birbal, as overseers.

In many stories, Birbal is portrayed as the guardian of the innocent. He solves criminal cases and convicts the guilty using his common sense and knowledge of human nature. Like Akbar, he does not rely on oaths and witnesses, but observes individuals closely and catches the inconsistencies in their testimonies.

The Tree Witness

One day, an old man came weeping and wailing to the Hall of Public Audience. 'Justice, Jahanpanah! I have been robbed in my old age! Only you can help me!'

Akbar looked at the man's grey hair and wrinkled face. He was bent over and frail and leaned on a staff. His faded turban and tattered garments showed that he was quite poor. 'Tell me your troubles, babaji,' the king said kindly. 'Birbal and I will try to help you.'

'Last year, before leaving on a long pilgrimage, I had left a bag of gold coins—my entire life's savings—with my neighbour for safekeeping. When I returned, he refused to give my money back. He claimed I had never given him any money at all. I am ruined! Who will take care of me in my old age, Jahanpanah?' The poor fellow began sobbing and crying all over again. If the king could not help him, he would have to beg for a living . . . or starve!

'Bring your neighbour to court tomorrow morning and Birbal will help me determine the truth,' the emperor said.

Next morning, the old man came to court with his neighbour, a strong young man with a big moustache.

'The old baba is mistaken, Your Majesty,' said the young man stroking his moustache. 'He is becoming forgetful in his old age. I am a rich man and an honest one. Why would I want to rob a poor old fellow, old enough to be my grandfather?'

Somehow, Birbal didn't quite trust the young neighbour. He turned to the old man. 'Did you have a witness, babaji? Did anyone see you giving the bag of gold to your neighbour?'

'No, Huzoor,' the old man said shaking his head sadly. 'I never thought I needed a witness. I trusted this young man as a son. Now I see I was mistaken.' His shoulders slumped in despair.

'Hmm . . . let me think,' said Birbal. 'Can you remember where you were, babaji, when you gave him this bag of coins?'

'Ah, that I do remember, Huzoor,' the old man said, brightening up. 'We were standing under a mango tree, in a mango grove outside our village. It was summer and the mangoes were ripe, and the air was filled with their delicious perfume.'

'A mango tree,' said Birbal delighted, clapping his hands. 'I thought you said you had no witness. That mango tree is your witness. Babaji, go immediately to the mango grove and ask the tree to come to court.'

A titter broke out among the nobles and other spectators. Everyone thought Birbal was joking. How could a mango tree come to court and give witness? A tree cannot walk or talk.

The old man was bewildered. But he was afraid to talk back to the king's minister, especially in front of all these richly dressed, important looking people. So he bowed low and left immediately for the mango grove.

An hour passed and the king and nobles were becoming restless. 'Be patient,' said Birbal. 'The old gentleman will be back any minute.'

'Oh no!' said the young neighbour, jumping up. 'He is not going to be back for several hours. He could not even have reached there yet!'

Birbal looked at the young man. 'Tell me, how far is the mango grove from here?'

'More than three miles away, Huzoor. But that old fellow walks so slowly, it will take him at least three hours to get there and back!'

'Very well, we shall wait,' said Birbal and proceeded with other business in the court.

Several hours later, the old man returned. He was dusty and weary and, of course, there was no tree with him. 'Thrice I repeated your order to the tree, Huzoor. But it would not budge. Now I am truly lost for I have no witness.' His face crumpled and his whole body shook with sobs.

'Don't worry, babaji,' said Birbal kindly. 'That mango tree has already borne witness for you.' He turned to the neighbour with an angry frown. 'You, young man, are a liar and a thief! You did take the old man's money under a mango tree. How else would you know which mango tree and how far away it was?'

The emperor and his courtiers burst into applause. Birbal had solved yet another case! The neighbour was ordered to give the old man not one bag of gold coins but two, and was then led away to jail. The old man went away singing the praises of Akbar and Birbal.

Whose Money Is It?

One day, as Birbal sat in court listening to cases, two men came in. One was an oil merchant and the other was a butcher. The butcher was clutching a cloth bag filled with coins. Each man claimed to be the owner of the money.

'Huzoor, I went to the butcher's shop to sell him some oil,' said the oil merchant. 'As I opened my bag to put in the coins, this greedy man was tempted by the sight of all the money and snatched my purse away. I shouted and collected people outside his shop and told them what had happened, but this rascal insists the money is his!'

Birbal turned to the butcher to hear his side of the story.

'It happened like this, Sire,' the butcher began. 'When the oil merchant came to my store to sell me oil, I left

my seat next to my money box and went inside to fetch a container for the oil. When I returned, I found my bag of coins missing from the box and saw the merchant disappearing around the corner. I ran after him and caught him, but the liar insists the bag is his!'

Birbal looked from one angry face to the other. Both men appeared to be telling the truth. It was difficult to tell which one was guilty.

People in court began to whisper amongst themselves. Birbal had quite a reputation for solving complex cases. But what would he do now?

Birbal picked up the bag of money and examined it closely. Then he sniffed it. 'Bring a vessel filled with hot water,' he ordered one of the court attendants.

When the water was brought in, Birbal poured the coins from the bag into the container. The coins sank to the bottom of the vessel, but soon drops of oil began to float upon the surface.

'Aha!' Birbal exclaimed triumphantly. 'The bag belongs to the oil merchant, since it is so oily. The butcher is the thief!'

The Widow and the Dishonest Brahmin

An old widow, who earned her living washing dishes and cleaning floors in people's homes, decided that she would go on a pilgrimage to the holy city of Benares. But there was one problem. She had saved five hundred gold coins carefully for many years so that she would not have to work in her old age, and she did not know where to leave the coins. She did not want to carry them with her, as there could be robbers and thieves on the road. At the same time, she did not want to leave them in her empty house. Her husband had died many years ago and she had no children or relatives.

She decided to go to a Brahmin who lived outside the city. He wore the orange robes of a holy man who had given up worldly matters. He sat all day meditating and praying under a banyan tree. He seemed very honest and trustworthy. She went to him and asked him to keep her money safely for her until she returned from her pilgrimage.

'O no, sister!' the holy man exclaimed. 'I have no use for worldly things like money. Please do not burden me with this responsibility. If someone steals your coins, you will blame me.'

But the old widow insisted that he help her. Finally, he agreed reluctantly. 'Very well. But you must stitch it into a bag and bury it here under the tree yourself. I will not even touch your money.'

Gladly, the widow hurried home and sewed her gold coins into a cloth bag. She then dug a hole under the banyan tree and buried her bag in it in front of the Brahmin. Thanking him profusely, she left on her journey to Benares.

'I will be back in six months and will relieve you of the responsibility,' she promised.

But six months went by and she did not return. After yet another six months had elapsed, the holy man began to think she had died on her journey. He thought about all the gold coins buried right under him. If he took all that money for himself, he could be a very rich man. After several days of thinking, he finally gave in to the temptation and dug up the bag. He unravelled the widow's stitches and took all the gold coins and replaced them with silver coins. Then he went to a tailor and had him stitch the bag back up. Pleased with himself, he hid the gold coins.

To his great dismay, almost two years after she had left, the old widow returned.

'I liked Benares so much that I could have stayed there for the rest of my life. If I had taken my money with me I would not even have come back. In fact, I may go back there once I have dug up the coins I left with you.'

Pretending that everything was fine, the Brahmin let the old woman dig up her bag and leave. She had so much faith in the Brahmin's honesty that she did not even look into the bag until a few days later. When she finally opened it, she was dreadfully shocked to find that instead of gold coins the bag now only contained silver coins of little value. She ran back to the Brahmin to complain.

'See, I knew that you would blame me if anything happened to your money. You stitched up the bag and buried it with your own hands. What do I know if your coins were gold or silver?' shrugged the Brahmin.

The widow wept and pleaded but it did not move the dishonest man one bit. She went to her neighbours and begged them to help her get her money back from the Brahmin. But no one had time to help a whining old woman. She sat in her hut in despair. All she could think of was how she would have to beg for a living in her old age because she had lost all her savings. She had no one to turn to. Then she suddenly thought of Birbal. Everyone said he was the champion of the poor and oppressed.

She hurried to the king's palace and told Birbal her story. Birbal carefully examined the bag that now contained silver coins. Some of the tailor's stitches were still intact.

'Is this your handiwork?' he asked in admiration. 'This is very professional stitching.'

The old woman looked closely at the stitches and shook her head. 'Alas, my eyesight is weak, and my stitches are big and clumsy.'

'Aha!' Birbal exclaimed. 'Then that rascally Brahmin replaced the gold coins with silver ones and had the opening sewed up by a professional tailor! Is there a good tailor in your city?'

That evening, Birbal took the bag to the tailor who worked in the area where the old widow lived. The tailor remembered sewing up a bag of silver coins for the Brahmin.

Birbal returned back to the palace with the old woman. He summoned the Brahmin and publicly accused him of stealing the widow's money. When the Brahmin insisted that he was innocent, Birbal told him that he had spoken to the tailor.

The Brahmin went pale. He confessed his crime and immediately produced the gold coins and returned them to the old widow. The old lady was overjoyed to have her hard-earned savings back.

The Magic Sticks

Once, a wealthy merchant came to seek his friend Birbal's advice. He had noticed that every now and then, a money bag or two would be missing from his storeroom. As the room had not been broken into, it was obvious that someone who was familiar with the house was stealing the money. It had to be one of his ten servants. But which one? The merchant was a kind man who could not bear to accuse any of his trusted men of stealing unless he was absolutely sure. If he complained to the authorities, they would arrest all ten men, and question and beat them until one of them confessed.

Birbal came to his rescue and promised to help him catch the thief. He accompanied the merchant to his home and asked him to assemble all his servants. In his hand he held a bundle of sticks, all of equal length. He gave one stick to each of the men.

'These are magic sticks,' he told the servants. 'Someone has been stealing money from this house. We do not believe that anyone of you is guilty, but these sticks will find the real thief. The stick that is held by the thief will grow one inch longer overnight. Tomorrow morning, when we compare the sticks, we will have the answer.'

The servants were led to separate rooms to spend the night. The next morning, Birbal examined each man's stick and measured them all. One stick turned out to be an inch shorter than the others. Birbal pounced on the owner.

'This is our thief! His stick is one inch shorter than the rest.'

'But ... but ...' the man blustered, 'you said that the guilty man's stick would *grow* one inch, not become shorter.'

'I said that because I knew that the guilty man would try to cut his stick short, thinking that it would grow one inch at night!' Birbal said triumphantly. 'By cutting the stick short, you revealed your guilt.'

The thief hung his head; he had nothing to say. The merchant was filled with admiration.

'Birbal, your common sense saved me from a good deal of trouble and these nine honest men from dishonour. No wonder the emperor prizes you as he does!'

THE KING

AND

HIS PEOPLE

Giving to his people was both a duty and a pleasure for Akbar. He was always looking for ways to help his subjects. He introduced an old Hindu custom into his court, where the king is weighed against valuable materials, which were donated to the poor. Since Muslims follow the lunar calendar and Akbar used the Persian system of measuring time by the sun, he had two birthdays. On his solar birthday, Akbar would be weighed twelve times against several commodities including gold, silk, perfumes, copper, butter, iron, seven kinds of grain and salt. According to the number of years he had lived, an equal number of goats, sheep and fowls were given away to people to breed. On his lunar birthday, Akbar was weighed against eight articles including silver, tin, cloth, lead, fruits, mustard oil and vegetables. This tradition was also adopted by later Mughal emperors.

But his birthday was not the only time the king

gave away donations. Every day, his clerks read out names of soldiers and guards who had never received a gift from the king, and Akbar donated horses to each person. Needy persons were supported with regular allowances. Stipends or grants of land were given to scholars, spiritual recluses and men of good birth who were unable to provide for themselves. He established eating houses for the poor. Gold and silver meant for charity was kept available in the public audience hall, and several bags of a thousand coins each were kept ready inside the palace as well.

Akbar also encouraged his nobles and courtiers to be generous and to donate a certain portion of their earnings to the poor. In October 1578 in Fatehpur, he had a large tank, which was about twenty yards long and three yards deep, emptied of water and filled with millions of coins, which he vowed to give away to holy men, scholars and the needy. The money was spent over three years.

Akbar liked to see for himself how people lived and whether or not they were happy in his kingdom. He did not want to rely on his officials for reports. He would disguise himself as an ordinary man and go into the streets of the city on his own. Thus he was able to observe people going about their everyday business without knowing that they were being watched by their emperor.

It is possible that Birbal sometimes accompanied him on such jaunts, but there is no evidence to say that he did. In the following story, Akbar carries his royal seal with him as he wanders about in disguise. In actual fact, the royal seal was always kept in the care of designated officials, not carried around on the king's person.

The Emperor's Disguise

Birbal did not approve of Akbar's habit of wandering about the streets of the city in disguise. 'A king is an important man. His life should be protected. Think of what would happen to your subjects if someone were to murder you on the street. The country would be in chaos. You have a responsibility to your people to look after yourself, Your Majesty,' he protested.

'Yes, Birbal,' agreed the emperor. 'But I also have a responsibility to look after my people. I cannot trust the reports of the officials. You know how corrupt some of them are. I have to see things with my own eyes. Besides, it's fun!'

Akbar donned a fake beard and the faded clothes of a poor traveller. He slipped out of the palace while Birbal looked on disapprovingly.

The disguised king wandered around in the city

bazaar. Pretending to be a traveller from a distant place, he asked the shopkeepers and other people he met questions about the state of affairs in the country.

By and by, he realized that someone was following him. From the corner of his eye, he could see a man with a long black beard and orange garments. He wore holy beads around his neck and carried a begging bowl. He seemed to be milling around aimlessly, but every time Akbar walked to a different shop, the holy man appeared in the background. Akbar tried to lose him by walking faster, but when he turned around, the holy man was still there. He must have walked just as fast.

Finally, Akbar decided to confront him. He stopped abruptly and walked up to the man. 'Who are you and what is your name?'

The man smirked and stroked his beard. 'My name is Wanderer.'

'What do you do?'

'I wander.'

'Where do you live?'

'Everywhere.'

The emperor began to lose patience with these cheeky answers. The man showed no respect. Akbar wanted to shake him out of his nonchalant attitude. 'Do you know who I am?'

The man smiled impudently. 'A human being just like me.'

For some reason, Akbar wanted to impress this man with his importance. 'I am the Emperor of Hindustan!'

'Oh, really?!' The man bowed in mock humility. Then he threw back his head and laughed. 'And I am the Emperor of the Universe! Now you bow to me.'

Akbar was determined to get some respect from this insolent rascal. He took his seal out from his cummerbund and held it out to the man. 'See with your own eyes. This is the royal seal. I use it to stamp all important documents. I really *am* the emperor.'

The man hesitated but still looked sceptical. He reached out and took the seal to examine it more closely. He held it close to his eyes. Then suddenly, he turned around and ran away before the surprised Akbar could stop him. He fled through the crowded bazaar, taking the royal seal with him.

'Stop! Thief! Catch that man!' Akbar ran after the saffron-robed scoundrel. By and by, a couple of strong men grabbed the thief.

'Let me go!' the thief commanded in an imperious voice. 'Can't you see I am the emperor?'

When his captors laughed at him, he held out the royal seal in his palm. 'See, I can prove it. This is the royal seal. Sometimes I wander about the city in disguise to see how my people are doing. Now off with all of you. Go back to your business.'

'A million pardons, Your Majesty!' Mumbling and bowing low, the people dispersed and the thief walked off.

Akbar watched all this from a hidden corner. Not having the seal to prove his identity, he was afraid to come out and challenge the thief. Ashamed of his carelessness in losing the royal seal, he walked back to the palace and slipped into his bedchamber.

Only Birbal could help him recover the seal, but he was embarrassed to tell him what had happened. After all, he had gone into the city against Birbal's advice. To his great surprise, he saw the royal seal lying by his bed, on top of a letter.

The letter was from Birbal: 'Your Majesty, now do you understand how dangerous it is for you to be wandering about the streets of the city without guards? This time you only lost your seal. Next time it could be your life.'

The relieved emperor laughed out loud. So that had been Birbal dressed as a beggar! No doubt, he had been trying to teach his king a lesson.

The Golden Touch

A soldier who had once served in the royal army died. His wife and widowed mother had no one to support them. Over the years, their savings dwindled and very little was left for the two women to live on. A neighbour suggested that they go to Birbal for advice. He was always willing to help the needy.

Birbal listened to their problems patiently. He told the old lady to appeal to the emperor for support. As Akbar was known for his generosity, he would certainly help them. But the old lady was too proud to ask for charity, even from the king.

'Very well, then,' said Birbal. 'Give His Majesty a gift. Something that has sentimental value, even if it is not expensive. If he is pleased, he will give you a gift in return. This is not begging. It will be an exchange of gifts.'

This idea pleased the old widow. The next day, she proceeded to Akbar's palace with her daughter-in-law. They were both dressed in their finest clothes. They did not wish to appear shabby and poor at this important occasion.

Birbal introduced the two women to the king. The old lady presented the heavy gift they had carried all the way from home. It was her son's sword.

'For twenty years, he fought in your army with this sword, Jahanpanah. Many an enemy did he kill with it. He was a loyal soldier and I want you to keep this as a token of his loyalty to you.'

Akbar took the weapon and examined it closely. It was old and rusty, and not of very good workmanship. It was of no use to him whatsoever, but since the soldier's old mother had presented it to him with so much love, he could not refuse it. He gave the sword to an attendant for safekeeping and asked the keeper of the treasury to give the two women five gold coins each. He could not send them back empty-handed, even though they were well dressed and appeared to be in no need for money.

Birbal was dismayed when he heard the small amount the emperor had decided to give as a gift. He jumped up. 'I would like to examine the sword, Your Majesty.'

Birbal took the sword and looked at it closely. Then

he turned it over and brought it up to his eyes, staring at every inch of the weapon. He did this several times, in silence, frowning as though puzzled. Akbar was surprised by his behaviour.

'Is something wrong, Birbal?'

'Oh, nothing is wrong, Your Majesty. I just thought . . . Let it be.'

'Speak what is on your mind, Birbal. You seem confused.'

Birbal shrugged. 'It's just that I was so sure the sword would have turned into gold.'

'The sword turning into gold . . . what are you talking about?'

'Well, Your Majesty, as you know, the alchemist's stone turns all it touches into gold. I was convinced that anything which was touched by your generous and benevolent hands would turn into gold . . .'

Akbar understood what Birbal was hinting at. He turned to the treasurer. 'Weigh this sword and give its weight in gold coins to the soldier's mother and his wife.'

Birbal smiled in satisfaction. The two women gratefully received their gift from the king and left the palace, a million blessings in their hearts for their wise and diplomatic benefactor, Birbal.

The Palms of Their Hands

One day, Akbar was in one of his thoughtful moods. This happened from time to time. The king liked to wonder about things: why is the sky so high, why can't deaf children talk, and so on.

Today he wondered out aloud, 'Birbal, why is it that no hair grows on my palms? I have hair on my arms, chest, face, everywhere—but none on the palm of my hands!'

As usual, the quick-witted Birbal had a ready answer. 'Your Majesty, you are always giving things away. Why, you sit here hour after hour and pass out coins to the poor and needy, as well as gifts to your officers and nobles. You are so generous, the palms of your hands are always in use; that is why no hair grows on them.'

Akbar was pleased with the answer but it did not satisfy him completely. He thought for a moment.

'Then why is it that no hair grows on *your* palms, Birbal?'

Birbal spread out his palms before the emperor. 'Jahanpanah, these worthless palms are always receiving gifts from you. This is why they do not have time to grow hair.'

Entertained by this line of reasoning, the emperor had one more question. He looked around at the other nobles.

'They why is it, Birbal, that none of these men have hair on their palms either? My treasury would be empty if I was as generous as you say.'

The other courtiers waited expectantly to see how Birbal would reply.

'Your Majesty, those who do not receive from you stand around wringing their hands in jealousy when they watch the good fortune of those of us who do. This is why no hair grows on their palms either.'

Akbar and everyone else burst out laughing. It was a ridiculous set of answers to an equally absurd set of questions.

The Obedient Husbands

One day, Akbar and Birbal were wandering through the streets of Agra disguised as ordinary men. Suddenly, as they were walking past a house, they heard a woman shouting and raging from within. They could not help hearing the angry words she was yelling.

'She must be screaming at one of her children,' said Akbar. 'Obviously, someone has made her furious.'

The next moment, the door of the house flew open and a man came stumbling out as though he had been pushed. His cap was thrown after him by a woman's hand.

'. . . and don't come back home until you get it right, you stupid man!' the same angry female voice continued. Then the door slammed shut. The man picked up his cap, dusted it off, placed it upon his head and walked away. He looked very dejected.

Birbal smiled. 'It wasn't her children she was yelling at, Your Majesty. It was her husband. It looks as though he is in a lot of trouble with his wife.'

The emperor was absolutely shocked. He could not believe that a man in his kingdom would allow his wife to treat him in such a manner. Surely his male subjects could not be that feeble!

'This man must be an exceptional coward. No other red-blooded, able-bodied man would allow his wife to speak to him so rudely,' he said.

Birbal coughed politely, the way he did when he was about to disagree with his king. 'A thousand pardons, Your Majesty, for not being able to agree with you. You are the Emperor of India—a powerful king. Men and women alike obey you and do your bidding. I cannot imagine any of *your* wives speaking to you with a raised voice . . . but for us ordinary men, it is quite a different matter.'

Akbar could not believe his ears. 'Are you telling me that this is not an exceptional case? Are you trying to tell me that most men in my kingdom are bullied by their wives?!'

'Not bullied, Your Majesty. But there is no question that our wives have a good deal of power and authority over us. We husbands know that if we want a good meal and peace in our homes, we had better listen to our wives.'

Akbar and Birbal continued to argue over the issue for several days. The emperor refused to believe that strong, capable men would allow their wives to order them around.

Finally, Birbal offered to put the matter to rest by conducting a poll. He invited all the married men in Agra to assemble in the palace yard. Hundreds of men collected there, wondering why they had been summoned.

Birbal stood up and addressed them. 'His Majesty would like to know how many of you good men obey your wives. Those who do, move to the left. Those who do not, move to the right.'

To Akbar's amazement, the entire crowd of men shuffled off to the left. So Birbal was right. All the married men in Agra obeyed their wives. All except one. One man stood alone, away from the crowd, on the right. Akbar was delighted to see that at least one man was brave enough to stand up to his woman.

'Birbal, bring that man to me. He is a hero. I must reward him for his courage. Apparently, all the other men in my kingdom are spineless cowards,' said the emperor.

Birbal brought the lone man to the king. 'His Majesty would like to know why, when all the other men moved

to the left, you remained alone on the right.'

The young man hung his head. 'My wife has always told me to stay away from crowds, Huzoor. So when all the men huddled together in one part of the yard, I moved to the other side.'

Birbal looked triumphantly at the emperor. This was, after all, yet another obedient husband. Akbar groaned.

MATTERS

OF

FAITH

Since childhood, Akbar had been very interested in spirituality and religion. When he was twenty years old, he visited the Chishti shrine of Sufi saints at Ajmer. Contact with the Sufi order had a powerful effect on the young emperor. He became very conscious of the sufferings of humanity. He abolished some laws and taxes that he felt were not humane and against the principles of Islam.

Akbar also began to visit Shaikh Salim Chishti, another widely respected Sufi who lived in a village called Sikri near Agra. Akbar was worried because he was by now over twenty-five years old and had several wives, but no male heir. Shaikh Salim predicted that the emperor would soon have three sons, a prediction which did indeed come true. In honour of Shaikh Salim, Akbar built a new capital city at Sikri along with a huge mosque, which soon became an important place of pilgrimage. Akbar named his new city Fatehpur

Sikri, the City of Victory.

Akbar was interested in other religions also besides Islam. He began to invite representatives from other religions to the debates at Fatehpur Sikri and at his palace. Zoroastrians, Hindus, Jains and Christians, all took part in the intense debates. Undoubtedly, Birbal would have participated in these discussions. He was probably responsible for introducing Hindu scholars and holy men to the emperor. He also taught the king a great deal about Hinduism, including some rituals that Akbar decided to follow. Akbar also showed great reverence towards the pictures of the Virgin Mary brought for him by the European Christian priests visiting his court. He donated land to the Christians to build a church and also gave the leaders of the Sikh religion land where they founded Amritsar, their holy city.

In 1582, Akbar started a new code of religious behaviour, which has come to be known today as *Din Illahi*. It combined elements from various religions, which Akbar felt were the most important. Birbal was the only Hindu courtier to become Akbar's disciple.

The Holy Man

Akbar liked everything to look perfect. The palace gardens and the public halls should always be neat and clean so that they could make a good impression on visitors, he said.

One day, as he was walking around the palace inspecting his land with pride, he saw a man taking a nap right in the middle of the garden under the shade of a tree. His ragged clothes were saffron, the colour worn by holy Hindu men. His beard and moustache were so shaggy that you could barely see his face. Akbar was irritated. This was no place for an unsightly beggar to rest! He went up to the man and ordered him to leave.

The man awoke from his sleep and stretched. Unconcerned by Akbar's air of authority, he asked, 'Why should I leave? Does the shade of this tree belong to you?'

'Of course it belongs to me!' said the infuriated emperor. 'So does the tree itself, the garden, the palace and everything in it, too.'

'How about the river—is that yours too?'

'Yes, this river and all the rivers in the kingdom belong to me. In fact, the whole of India belongs to me! I am the emperor.'

The saffron-clad intruder pondered this for a while. He was still not impressed by Akbar's importance. 'And before you were born, who did all of this belong to?'

'My father, of course!'

'And before him?'

Akbar began to understand what the man was getting at. He dropped his arrogant attitude and sat down on the grass next to the holy man.

'The kingdom belonged to my grandfather before my father.'

The holy man gestured at the palace and its surroundings. 'So, like them, you will possess all these beautiful things during your life and afterwards they will pass on to your son and then to his son?'

'That is true,' agreed the emperor, now deep in thought. 'These possessions are mine only temporarily. I own them only while I am on this earth. Then they pass on to someone else.'

'Exactly!' said the holy man with a wise smile. 'All material things are temporary. No one really owns the shade of a tree or a rest house.'

Akbar, who was quite fond of musing about the meaning of life, said thoughtfully, 'The whole world is like a rest house. We all stay here for a while and then move on, is that what you are trying to tell me?'

'You are correct, Your Majesty! Being arrogant about one's material possessions is false pride.' Akbar looked up, startled at the change in the holy man's tone. He recognized the familiar voice.

'Birbal! I should have known it was you. Always provoking me to think further and deeper, aren't you?!' The holy man stood up laughing and peeled off his shaggy false beard. He made a deep bow to the smiling emperor.

'It was my privilege and duty, King of the World, to remind you of the true meaning of life. Vanity and arrogance are not becoming of a great mind like yours.'

The Holy Name of Rama

Akbar had made it his business to learn all about the Hindus and their holy books. He even had the Ramayana, the story of Rama translated and read to him. He knew so much, he was beginning to feel all-powerful.

One day, he called Birbal and said, 'Birbal, you Hindus write the name of Rama at the top of all your writings. I am going to pass an order today, that from now on, they should write my name instead of Rama.'

Birbal pondered the matter. 'It is indeed a wonderful idea, Your Majesty, but remember one thing. When the name of Rama is uttered, even stones will float on water. So much power and magic does that word have. Are you sure that stones will float on water when your name is mentioned?'

Akbar decided to drop the idea. He did not want to appear weaker than Rama.

IN THE DURBAR

IN THE DURBAR

Rulers were usually surrounded by professional flatterers—bards and poets—who would constantly remind the king of his greatness and sing his praises. The court poets were usually learned men, who were well versed in the technicalities of poetry, grammar and literature. They also knew a great deal about politics, warfare and history, and were practised in the art of polished and ornate expression. Kings would handsomely reward the poets who pleased them the most.

Since most people could not read and write, their only way of learning about the present and past happenings in the kingdom was through the songs of bards and storytellers. Bards were known as *bhats* in northern India. Like newspaper and television reporters today, they told the common man what the king was doing. Thus, the ruler's reputation to a great extent depended on what the bards were saying about him.

As a result, kings usually treated the bards with great respect. Bards were usually well educated, especially skilled in the arts of music and poetry.

Another group of people who got a lot of importance at Akbar's court were artists. Art was extremely important to Akbar and his ancestors from Central Asia and Persia. Akbar had famous artists set up painting workshops for his court, which could include up to a hundred painters of different nationalities. He had many books—storybooks, religious works and histories—illustrated by these men. Often several people worked on a single painting, each specializing in a certain skill. Akbar was particularly interested in portraits, especially those that were true to life; he ordered portraits to be made of all the important nobles at his court, including Birbal.

In keeping with the traditions of his ancestors, Akbar greatly valued knowledge, learning and fine books. Books were precious commodities as they had to be copied by hand. Akbar built up a library of 24,000 books including rare and precious manuscripts that he had either inherited, won in battle or commissioned. He also established a Bureau of Translations where books in various languages were translated into Persian, including major Hindu books such as the Ramayana, the Mahabharata and the Harivamsa (Krishna's life).

There were many scholars at Akbar's court who were proficient in more than one language, such as Badauni, who did a lot of translation work. Birbal, too, spoke fluent Persian as well as Hindi and Sanskrit. He is credited with translating the Bhagavad Gita.

Akbar's other interests included pigeon-flying and *chaughan*, a form of polo. Birbal too enjoyed playing polo.

Mother Tongue

At Akbar's court, there were many scholars learned in more than one language. Some knew Arabic, the language of the holy Koran. Others spoke Turki, the language of Akbar's ancestors. There were men who understood Sanskrit, in which the Hindu holy books are written. Of course, everyone spoke Persian, the official language of the court.

One day, a traveller arrived at Akbar's palace. He spoke Arabic, Persian, Turki, Sanskrit and even Chinese and Latin. The king's scholars were astonished by his linguistic abilities. He could hold a fluent conversation with them in any of the languages in which they specialized. No one could detect any mistakes or even the trace of an accent in his speech.

Akbar was impressed by this talented stranger and wanted to know more about him. 'Which country are you from originally? What is your mother tongue?'

But the mysterious stranger would not tell. 'That is for me to know, and you to find out!'

Akbar turned to Birbal. 'Birbal, surely you have guessed by now where this man is from.'

Birbal had been observing and listening to the newcomer closely since he had arrived, but he said, 'I need a little more time, Your Majesty. You will know by tomorrow.'

That night, Birbal, accompanied by one of his servants, went to the stranger's room secretly. He hid himself near the bedroom window, while his servant went in and sprinkled some cold water on the sleeping man. Startled, the man awoke and exclaimed in an angry voice. When he went back to sleep, Birbal and his servant returned quietly to their home.

The next morning, Birbal announced to the emperor:

'Your Majesty, our mysterious friend is from Gujarat.'

The stranger was speechless in amazement. 'But … but how did you know?!'

Birbal smiled. 'Forgive me, Stranger, but I startled you in your sleep last tight. Unwittingly, you yelled out some Gujarati words. No matter how many languages they may speak, when surprised or in pain, men usually use their mother tongue.'

Akbar and the other courtiers broke into applause as the stranger bowed to Birbal in admiration.

A Long Story

Akbar loved to listen to stories. He hired readers whose only work was to read aloud books to the king. He especially loved exciting tales full of danger and action. If he had had a hard day hunting or riding, he would sometimes fall asleep and start snoring before the story was over. Then the reader would quietly snuff out the lamp and leave the royal bedchamber. But if the king had spent the day doing tedious and boring things, then he would be wide awake and alert at bedtime, waiting to be entertained.

On one particular night, it was Birbal's turn to tell Akbar a story. The king was in the mood for a really long story while Birbal was tired and sleepy. But, naturally, Birbal could not back out of his duties to his royal master. He stifled his yawn and began to spin a yarn.

'I've already heard this one, Birbal. Tell me a new one.'

Birbal racked his brains to think of a tale he had not already told Akbar. His tired mind could not come up with anything. He decided to make up a story on the spot and also cure Akbar of this tedious habit.

'Once upon a time,' Birbal began, 'a farmer had a granary made where he could store the grain harvested from his field. It was important that the shed be absolutely airtight without any opening, so that the grain would remain fresh. But after the granary had been built and the wheat had been stored, one small problem remained.'

Akbar sat up in bed. 'What was that?' he asked eagerly. Perhaps the story would turn out to be an exciting one.

'Well, the builders didn't do a really good job,' Birbal continued. 'A tiny hole remained at the top of the shed. It was large enough to allow a sparrow to enter. The bird carried off a grain of wheat. It told the other sparrows about it. Next, one more sparrow came and took a grain in its beak.'

'Then what happened?' asked the emperor.

'Another sparrow came and carried off a grain of wheat.'

'And then?'

'One more sparrow flew off with a grain of wheat from the granary.'

'But what happened next?'

Birbal described how each bird carried away a grain of wheat. By the time he had repeated the same sentence fifty times, Akbar had become really impatient. 'But I want to know what happened next in the story! I've heard enough about the sparrows.'

'But, Your Majesty, thousands and thousands of birds came to that granary and carried off a grain of wheat in their beaks. I have only told you about a few. The story cannot move on until every single grain of wheat has been removed. It may take several months or years to complete this story.'

'Enough, enough!' grumbled the disgruntled king. 'I don't want to hear any more of this boring tale. Leave me alone. I want to sleep.'

Happy to be relieved of his duty, Birbal snuffed out the lamp and tiptoed out of the emperor's bedroom.

The Five Greatest Fools in Agra

Akbar was tired of the endless debates in his court. He was sick of listening to wise men and scholars. They were so serious and boring. He wanted to have some fun for a change. He decided he wanted to listen to some fools instead.

Akbar summoned Birbal. 'Tomorrow morning, I want you to go into Agra and find me the five biggest fools in the city. Bring them to my palace by the end of the day.'

Birbal was neither surprised nor taken aback by this strange request. He knew the king was in a strange mood. He knew better than to argue with him. He bowed low, and touched his head with his right palm, as was the customary greeting for servants to the king. 'But of course, Your Majesty. Your wish is my command. By the end of the day tomorrow, you will have your five fools.'

Next morning, at sunrise, Birbal set off for the city. He didn't have any idea of how to find fools. He decided to walk around in the more crowded part of the town. The more people there were to look at, the better were his chances of finding a fool. He sat down in a corner of the bazaar and waited.

Before long, he saw a curious sight. Along came a woodcutter, seated on a donkey, carrying a bundle of wood on his head. He could have strapped it behind him on the donkey.

Birbal hastened to the woodcutter's side. 'Excuse my curiosity, sir, but could you tell me why you carry your burden on your head, when you have such a fine donkey to carry it for you?'

The woodcutter was delighted to have such a refined gentleman address him, a mere woodcutter, as 'sir'.

'This good donkey has worked for me all his life. Now he is old and feeble. I do not wish to give him too heavy a load to bear. So, although I sit on his back, I carry the wood I have chopped on my own head.'

Birbal stifled a smile. Here was his first fool. He said to the man, 'How wonderful to meet a man as kind as you in these otherwise cruel times. Although he is a beast of burden, you share your donkey's load. How lucky he is to have a master like you. Come with me,

kind sir, and I will make sure that neither you nor your donkey carries a heavy load ever again.'

The woodcutter, pleased to be getting so much attention from the polite gentleman, readily agreed to follow him around town. So, Birbal, the woodcutter and his donkey wandered about looking for more fools.

Suddenly Birbal stopped short. There in the middle of the path in front of them lay a man, flat on his back. He was cycling his legs in the air and he held both his arms straight up and stiffly apart.

Birbal went up to the man. 'What are you doing lying on the ground like that? Our donkey almost stepped upon you. Why don't you stand up?'

'Help me to stand up,' the man gasped. 'I slipped and fell and now I cannot rise without using my hands.'

'Then why don't you use your hands to help yourself? Why do you hold them up in the air like that?'

'Questions, questions,' grumbled the man. 'Are you going to help me up or not?'

'Very well,' said Birbal, and pulled the man to his feet. He continued to hold his arms straight out in front of him.

'You must tell me why you hold your arms in that position,' Birbal insisted, his curiosity thoroughly aroused.

'Well, sire, this morning my wife sent me to the bazaar to buy a measure of cloth. This is how much cloth she wants me to buy,' the man said, emphasizing the distance between his hands. 'If I put my arms down, how will I remember how much cloth she wanted? You don't know my wife, sire. She would not be pleased if I did not buy the right amount of fabric.'

'Aha!' Birbal exclaimed, highly entertained by the story and happy to have found another fool. 'So that is the reason for your strange posture. How fortunate your wife is to have a husband that obeys her so well. Come with me today, and your wife will have as much fabric as her heart desires for the rest of her life.'

And the dutiful husband happily joined Birbal and the woodcutter as they walked through the city looking for more fools. But fools weren't that easy to come by. Most people in Agra were quite clever. The day passed, it started getting dark, and Birbal still hadn't found another fool.

Suddenly, he saw a strange sight. By the flaming torch which served as street lighting, was a full grown man, crawling about on his hands and knees like a baby. This looked very promising!

Birbal ran up to the man. 'What are you doing crawling around in the dust like that, good sir? Your fine white silken clothes will get all messed up!'

The man, who looked as though he were a prosperous merchant, looked up. 'I lost my diamond ring when I was chatting with some friends this afternoon. I have a habit of twisting it about on my finger, and it must have fallen off. I only just discovered my loss and came back to look for it.'

'A diamond ring!' exclaimed Birbal. 'It must have been quite expensive. Perhaps we can all help you look for it. Do you remember exactly where you were standing when you were chatting with your friends?'

Pleased with the attention of the sympathetic stranger, the merchant pointed to a clump of trees a short distance away. 'We were standing under the shade of the trees in the hot afternoon.'

Birbal was astonished. 'If you lost your ring there under the trees, then why are you looking for it here, so far away?'

The merchant was quite irritated by Birbal's failure to understand the obvious. 'It is completely dark under the trees. How do you expect me to find a small ring in the dark?! I am looking for it under the streetlight because I can see clearly here.'

Birbal struck his forehead with his palm. 'But of course! How foolish of me to ask such a silly question! But, noble sir, you seem tired and dusty. Accompany me and I shall obtain for you not one diamond ring, but two.'

The merchant agreed to go with Birbal. He had looked long enough for his ring, and now he might get two for free. He had nothing to lose.

Birbal was exhausted by now with his day-long excursion in the city. He turned towards the palace with his three fools.

One by one, he presented the fools to the emperor. Akbar laughed heartily when he heard each one's story. He gave each man two handfuls of gold coins, more than enough to buy what Birbal had promised them. He was about to reward Birbal, when he stopped short.

'Birbal, I asked you for five fools. But you have only brought me three. Where are the other two fools?'

Birbal bowed his head and humbly touched it with his right palm. 'Your Majesty, the fourth fool is I, for having gone on such a foolish mission.'

Akbar stifled a smile. He could see what Birbal was getting at. 'And the fifth fool, Birbal. Dare I ask who the fifth fool is?'

At this Birbal prostrated himself flat on the floor, and placed the emperor's feet upon his head. Then he kissed the royal feet and stood up.

'May the sun and the moon revolve around you! May you live for a thousand years! May the world sing your praises for another ten thousand years! But if

Your Majesty will forgive this worthless servant's impertinence—may I dare to humbly suggest, that the fifth fool is *you* for having sent me on such a foolish mission.'

Akbar laughed until the tears ran down his cheeks. Then he clasped Birbal to him in a big embrace. 'This is why I love you, Birbal. You can make me laugh and forget for a moment how important I am!'

The Perfect Portrait

Many of Akbar's nobles were inspired by the emperor's interest in painting. They also employed artists to paint pictures and portraits for them. Many gifted and talented painters worked in Akbar's capital.

One day, a noble asked a young painter at court to paint an exact likeness of him. The painter was not that well known as yet and wanted an opportunity to impress important people at court with his work. He hoped that the emperor would then give him a chance to work on a more important project. He was delighted to have been approached, and quickly painted a portrait of the noble and brought it back to him.

He found that the noble had just shaved off his beard. 'What sort of a portrait is this? I asked for an exact likeness! Look at me—do I have a beard?'

'But you did when you sat for the portrait, sire,' the

artist countered.

The noble would not be appeased. Afraid that he would be considered incompetent, the painter immediately agreed to redo the picture. This time, when he presented the completed portrait, the noble had just shaved off his moustache.

'Is this what you call an exact likeness?! Do I have a moustache?'

It was pointless to argue that he had had a moustache when he sat for the portrait. The poor painter redid the picture. Five times, he painted the noble's portrait. Five times the noble changed his appearance in some way so that the painting would not be an exact likeness of him. The struggling young artist became sad and frustrated. It appeared his career at court would be ruined by this capricious noble. He went to Birbal and asked for his help.

Birbal listened to the whole story. He suggested that the painter ask for one last chance. He then told him how to teach the man a lesson. This time, when he went to present the completed portrait to the noble, Birbal accompanied him. As the noble waited smugly, ready to pounce on some inaccuracy, the artist handed him a mirror.

'What is this? This is not a painting! It is just a mirror.'

'Precisely, sire. The only way you can obtain an exact likeness of yourself is if you look at yourself in the mirror. You do not need an artist. There is no art involved.'

Shamefaced, the noble had to concede that the young man was indeed a talented artist and had to pay him for all the portraits he had painted of him. Thanks to Birbal, the painter's reputation was saved. He even went on to become quite well known as a portrait painter.

The Flatterer

One day, a poet from a distant place arrived at Akbar's court. The king was interested in traveller's tales and also enjoyed fine poetry. He was so pleased with the visitor's songs and poems that he gave him a rich reward—a huge bag of gold. The poet was so overwhelmed by the king's generosity that he begged permission to compose a poem in his praise.

'You are the greatest king in Hindustan, Your Majesty. No other king in this land has a kingdom as big as yours, a heart as generous!'

Akbar smiled, quite pleased. He knew this was true. He was definitely the most important king in India in those days.

The flatterer continued, bowing low as he spoke. 'In fact, you are the greatest king in this world, Your Majesty. No other king in the world has a kingdom as powerful as yours. No other emperor has as many palaces or as magnificent a court as yours!'

Akbar nodded and smiled. Although he had not seen the world, he had visitors from other lands attend his court and he knew that his fame had spread far and wide. He was pleased at the flatterer's words. Everyone in the court was listening, including some foreign visitors. He decided to bestow an even greater reward on his eloquent admirer.

Pleased at the effect he was having on emperor, the poet continued. 'In fact, Your Majesty, the sun and the moon and the stars revolve around you ... because you are the greatest king in the universe—greater even than Lord Indra!'

He had gone too far. There was a stunned silence in the court. Lord Indra was the king of all gods, the highest god for Hindus. All the nobles—Hindus and Muslims, as well as the foreign visitors who were Christians—believed that no man could rival the greatness of God. Akbar, too, was taken aback by the man's words. But he was amused by the shocked looks on all the faces around him.

He looked around the hall. 'Well, what do you all think? Am I greater than God? No one is contradicting the man. Does that mean you agree with him?'

The nobles began to shift and shuffle uncomfortably.

They did not wish to be blasphemous. Yet, how could they tell the emperor without offending him that neither he nor any man was greater than God?

'If you agree that I am greater than God, then give me one reason why you think so.'

Akbar looked at his courtiers turn by turn. The men either lowered their eyes or coughed to hide their embarrassment. No one had the courage to answer his question truthfully and risk his displeasure.

Akbar turned to Birbal. 'Well, Birbal. Do you think I am greater than God?'

Unhesitatingly, Birbal replied, 'Undoubtedly, Your Majesty! Of course you are greater than God!'

'And why is that, Birbal?'

'Your Majesty, there is certainly one thing that you can do, that God cannot.'

'And what is that, Birbal?' Akbar waited eagerly to see what Birbal would say. The other nobles watched to see how Birbal would get himself out of this embarrassing situation without offending the emperor.

'Majesty, it you wish to banish a man, all you have to do is send him out of your kingdom. But if God, whose kingdom is the universe, wishes to banish a man ... He has nowhere to send him! Therefore, I repeat, Your Majesty, you are greater than God, because you can do one thing that He cannot do.'

Akbar was pleased at the tactful way Birbal had put him in his place. By reminding him that his kingdom had limits, while God's kingdom had none, Birbal had pointed out the infinite superiority of the Creator, but without insulting his emperor.

Akbar laughed delightedly. The nobles smiled and nervously wiped the sweat off their faces. Birbal had saved them all from a very tricky situation.

IN THE FAMILY

IN THE FAMILY

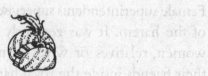

The kings who ruled Delhi before the Mughals had large numbers of wives living in strict seclusion in special parts of the palace called the harem. They had to veil themselves in front of males other than their husbands and close relatives. This practice of veiling was known as *parda*.

Akbar also had an enormous harem. It is said that he had more than 300 wives, though less than a dozen are mentioned by name in the history books of the time. Many of the marriages were political alliances with other royal families to ensure peace and harmony among the rulers. Akbar married at least six Hindu princesses for this reason.

Akbar's harem contained more than 5000 women. But not all of these were the king's wives or concubines. Other women related to the royal family—widowed aunts, unmarried sisters and cousins—also lived there along with their many maids. Each wife had a separate apartment and received a salary for her expenditure. Female superintendents supervised the different sections of the harem. It was zealously guarded. When other women, relatives or wives of nobles, wished to visit their friends inside the royal harem, they had to apply for permission.

Women had opportunities to learn languages such as Persian and Sanskrit, as well as art and fine literature. Parties of royal women went on pilgrimages every month. They also frequently accompanied the king on his travels to distant lands.

Royal women lived in a world of their own. Although they could not be seen by other men, they could observe a great deal from behind screened walls. They also had direct access to the king, who spent at least a few hours every day in the harem, and could influence his decisions. The king's mother was exceptionally important and had a higher position than his chief wife.

Royal children were especially pampered and coddled by the many loving females around them, not just their own mothers. Queens had many helpers and did not physically have to take care of their babies. Akbar had many wet nurses, or *anagahs*, when he was born. When he was separated from his parents for two years as a toddler, it was his nurses who looked after him.

When Akbar was four years, four months and four days old, he was scheduled to start his schooling at an auspicious hour chosen by astrologers, but he was nowhere to be found; he had run off to play! Akbar's father Humayun appointed teacher after teacher as he grew older, but the young prince was just not interested in studying. He preferred to spend his time flying pigeons, observing animals and hunting.

Yet, Akbar showed the signs of being an imperious ruler even as a child. His admirers claimed that by remaining unschooled, Akbar had been able to nurture the greatness within him. He did learn to read eventually but never liked to write himself. Despite his initial resistance to education, he later developed a tremendous respect for knowledge and gathered many learned scholars about him.

Appeasing the Begum

One of Akbar's wives had a brother that she doted on. She felt that he was one of the most capable men at court. And yet, her husband, the emperor, did not give him a position worthy of his qualities. Instead Birbal seemed to get undue favours and importance. She decided to take the matter up with her husband one more time.

'But, Begum,' the king pleaded, 'I need intelligent men running the affairs of the country. Your brother is a good man, but he just doesn't have what it takes to hold a really important position.'

'How about Birbal?' she countered. 'You just like him because he is funny. How can you justify entrusting a mere jester with such important responsibilities?'

'Birbal is not a mere jester, as you put it, Begum,' the king explained patiently. 'He is a very wise and intelligent man. He is so clever that I truly doubt there is anything he cannot do.'

The begum saw her chance. 'Very well, let us set Birbal an impossible task. If he is unable to perform it, then you give his position at court to my brother.'

Akbar did not wish to displease his pretty wife. She was his current favourite and he did not want her to sulk. Besides, he was completely confident that Birbal could do anything. 'Anything to please you, my pretty one. You suggest the task Birbal should perform.'

'Tomorrow when you are strolling in the garden, ask Birbal to fetch me. I will refuse to come. He will fail for sure.' She smiled triumphantly. Already she could imagine her brother being appointed as an important man at court.

The next day, the emperor was taking his evening stroll in the garden. He turned to Birbal and said, 'My begum is angry with me and refuses to see me. Please go and persuade her to join me. Only you can put her in a better mood.'

As Birbal turned to leave and do his king's bidding, the emperor added: 'Oh, and, Birbal, I should tell you that if you do not succeed in bringing her to me, I will have to give your post to the begum's brother. That would please her immensely.'

Birbal immediately understood what had happened.

He never underestimated the power of the women in the harem. Thank goodness the emperor had warned him. Birbal knew that Akbar could not stand the begum's brother, and would never want him in his circle of trusted advisors, but he must have been forced by his wife into making a promise. Birbal realized he had to make sure the begum went to see the emperor. His job depended on it.

He arrived in the harem and asked to be presented to the begum. The begum, of course, was waiting for him. She was eager to see him fail.

Birbal bowed low. 'Your Highness, I have an important message for you from the emperor. He is in the palace garden and wants you to . . .'

Just then, a servant entered and went up to Birbal. He whispered something in his ear. The begum could not hear what he said, but three words caught her attention: 'she is beautiful'.

Birbal's expression changed to one of embarrassment. He sent the servant away and turned to the begum. 'Things have changed, Your Highness. Please do not bother to come to the garden. His Majesty has other things to attend to.' He bowed and quickly left the room.

When he had gone, the begum began to worry. Why had Akbar changed his mind about inviting her

to the garden? Those three words she had overheard—
'she is beautiful'—troubled her greatly. Could it be
that the king was meeting another beautiful woman in
the garden? She was his favourite at the moment, but
the begum knew how easily the emperor could shift
his attention to another woman. The harem was full of
women who no longer interested the king. The begum
did not want to become one of them. She decided that
she would not allow another woman to take away her
place beside the emperor.

Hurriedly, the begum made her way to the garden,
where Akbar waited alone. He raised his eyebrows in
surprise. 'But, Begum, you swore that you would not
come when I called you. What made you change your
mind?'

The begum looked around the garden. Besides the
king's attendants, there was no one else present. No
beautiful woman. She realized that Birbal had fooled
her by making her jealous.

'Your Birbal tricked me into coming here,' she said
furiously.

'Did he tell you a lie? If he did, I will punish him.'

But Birbal had managed to manipulate her without
actually telling a lie. Just through the power of suggestion
he had shrewdly used her innermost fears to make her
jealous and arouse her curiosity. But the begum could

not admit to the emperor that she had been tricked into coming because she thought he was meeting another woman.

Birbal appeared a few minutes later and saluted the king and queen. Akbar smiled happily, relieved that he would not have to put up with the begum's insufferably pompous brother after all. 'Bravo, Birbal. I always said you could accomplish the impossible!'

The queen looked at the ground and said nothing. Reluctantly, she had to admit that Birbal was intelligent, with a deep understanding of human nature.

The Powers of Children

One morning, Birbal arrived late in court. The emperor had been waiting impatiently for him. 'Why are you late, Birbal? You know I do not like to be kept waiting.'

'A million apologies, Your Majesty! Normally I never allow anything to keep me from my duties. But today . . . well, it was just unavoidable.'

Akbar wouldn't let it go at that. His curiosity was aroused. 'But what happened, Birbal? What was important enough to keep you from your king?'

Surprisingly, Birbal, who always had a smooth and prompt answer for everything, seemed embarrassed. He didn't want to discuss the matter in front of the other nobles. But when Akbar persisted in probing, he finally admitted: 'Well, Majesty, it was my little grandson. His toy was broken and he wouldn't let me leave the house until I had fixed it for him.'

Akbar was flabbergasted. 'You allowed a mere child to get the better of you! Why, you are an adult! Surely you could have reasoned with him and explained that you would fix it later.'

'But, Majesty, one can't reason with a little child who is throwing a tantrum. Children are powerful creatures. They can humble the greatest adults if they wish.'

Akbar was not convinced. 'Bring your grandchild to court this minute. I will show you how to handle him.'

Birbal obediently fetched his two-year-old grandson into the emperor's presence. The toddler smiled sweetly at the king, and even agreed to come and sit in his lap.

Akbar looked triumphantly at Birbal. 'See how well I handle him. I have many grandchildren of my own.'

Then the boy began to fidget and shift. 'I'm hungry now,' he said, looking up at the king.

'What would you like to eat?' the emperor asked kindly.

The child thought for a moment. 'Sugar cane,' he said.

Attendants immediately brought in sugar cane that had been cut into tiny child-sized pieces.

The toddler refused to eat any of it. 'No-no, not like that, I want the big sugar cane.'

Akbar snapped his fingers and his servants brought in a large stick of sugar cane that had not been cut up. But even this did not please the child.

He began to sniffle. 'I want all the little pieces to be put back together to make a big one, like it used to be.'

'But that is impossible, child!' The emperor was beginning to get impatient. 'No one can join together a sugar cane that has been chopped up.'

'That's what I want. I will eat only that. Put it back together again this instant.' The boy stamped his foot and began to cry.

Desperately, the emperor tried to comfort him and distract him with other foods. Plates and plates of colourful and delicious sweets were brought in for the child. Then all kinds of fruits. But the child wouldn't have any of it. His wails grew louder and louder.

Akbar threw up his hands in defeat and handed the crying child back to his grandfather. 'I suppose you were right, Birbal. You cannot reason with small children, and therein lies their power. They can humble even the greatest adults.'

A Suitable Punishment

Before leaving for court one morning, Akbar was playing with one of his grandsons. The mischievous child pointed at his grandfather's moustache.

'Oh look, Baba, there is something stuck on your moustache. Let me brush it off.'

Akbar bent down and the lad quickly plucked out a hair from the king's moustache.

'Ouch!' It hurt! Akbar tried to catch the naughty fellow as he ran laughing out of reach.

Akbar was still thinking of this incident when he caught sight of Birbal in court that morning. He decided to trip his witty friend by asking him a trick question.

Akbar addressed all his nobles solemnly. 'This morning, some rascal plucked a hair from my moustache. What do you think would be a suitable punishment for such behaviour?'

The nobles were horrified to think that someone could do such a thing to the emperor. A chorus of responses arose.

'The culprit should be whipped fifty times!'

'Certainly, the death sentence for such a close attack on the king!'

'Each and every hair in his own moustache should be plucked out one by one as punishment.'

But Birbal said nothing. The emperor looked at him. 'Well, Birbal, what do you think would be a suitable punishment?'

'I think Your Majesty should catch the rascal, spank him and then give a big hug and a kiss.'

The nobles looked at Birbal in amazement.

'Now, why so lenient a punishment, Birbal? Do you think a person should be allowed to get away with an attack on the emperor's body?'

Birbal smiled. 'Only one of the emperor's own grandchildren would be able to get close enough to him to do such a thing. Only a little prince would have the impudence to pull a hair from his royal grandfather's moustache.'

The emperor laughed. Birbal had seen through his trick question.

THE KING'S

AMBASSADOR

Kings seldom called on each other in person because travel was tedious and dangerous. Instead, they sent important men in the kingdom as ambassadors to convey their messages. To show respect for each other, they would send lavish gifts.

Akbar sent Birbal on several diplomatic missions, especially to Hindu kings and chieftains. With his wit and charm, Birbal could accomplish what armies could not.

On one occasion, Birbal was sent to his former employer, the Raja of Rewa. Although the Raja had accepted Akbar's superiority and had sent his son to the Mughal court, he had never come to pay his respects to the emperor in person. Akbar took this to be a sign of disobedience and was about to send an army against him, but was persuaded that the Raja was just too timid to make the long journey on his own. Akbar sent Birbal to soothe the Raja's fears and bring him into the court. The Raja brought magnificent rubies as a gift for the emperor. Birbal's diplomacy thus averted a war.

The Raja of Dungarpur (a Rajput kingdom) wanted Akbar to marry his daughter, but was hesitant to send her to the royal harem. Birbal was sent with another noble to Dungarpur. He calmed the Raja's fears and escorted the princess safely to the emperor.

As it was well known that Birbal was close to the emperor, people would seek him out when they needed help at the court. The Raja of Kajli, a kingdom in south India, sent an ambassador to Akbar with a special healing knife as a gift. For a long time the ambassador was unable to get an introduction to the emperor. Finally, he appealed to Birbal, who presented him to Akbar. The healing knife was duly received by the king. It is claimed that more than two hundred sick people were eventually cured by touching the knife. At another time, Bhupat Chohan, a rebel, came to Birbal in order to obtain forgiveness from the emperor. Birbal was also sent to appease Masum Khan Farankhudi who had rebelled against the emperor.

Who is the Real Shah?

The Shah of Persia had heard of Birbal and his cleverness in solving problems. He wanted to see this man in action, so he asked his cousin, the Emperor of Hindustan, to send Birbal to Persia for a visit. Akbar was only too happy to send Birbal to Persia, loaded with many fine gifts for the Shah.

When Birbal arrived at the Persian capital, he was ushered into the Shah's audience chamber. To his surprise, there were seven men, all dressed in rich robes and all seated on thrones. It was impossible to tell who the real Shah was. All seven looked identical.

Birbal understood immediately that the Shah wanted to test him to see if he could identify the real Shah. Birbal looked carefully at the seven men. Then carefully and deliberately, he positioned himself in front of the man who was third from the left. He bowed deeply, touching his head with his right palm, which was the customary form of greeting, 'Your Majesty, the Emperor of Hindustan sends you his greetings and compliments. I have brought with me rich gifts as a token of his regard for you.'

The Shah gasped in surprise. 'You are truly as clever as they say, Birbal. But tell me, how did you know that I was the real Shah? You have never seen me before.'

'It was easy, Your Majesty. All the other men were looking at you, because you are their king. You alone had the assurance of authority. You looked straight at me.'

The Shah was truly impressed with this demonstration of Birbal's quick wits. He enjoyed his company and his humour for several weeks before he sent him back to India, loaded with presents for his cousin, Emperor Akbar.

Birbal Travels to Burma

Hussain Khan was always fretting that he was not being treated fairly by the emperor. Alter all, his sister was married to Akbar. Shouldn't he have a more important position at court than that good-for-nothing commoner Birbal? Birbal was always travelling here and there as ambassador. Surely Hussain Khan could handle important diplomatic missions just as well, if not better. Once more, he had his sister appeal to the emperor on his behalf.

Akbar was weary of Hussain Khan's constant whining. It would be wonderful to get rid of him for some time. One morning, he summoned both Hussain Khan and Birbal to his presence. He gave them a sealed scroll. 'I want both of you to go to the kingdom of Burma and deliver my letter to the king personally. It is a very important matter. You must wait for his answer before you return.'

Hussain Khan was delighted to get something important to do at last. He was not so happy that he had to share the assignment with Birbal, but then it would be nice to have a companion on the long journey to Burma. He insisted that being the emperor's brother-in-law, he should be the one to make a formal speech and present Akbar's letter to the king of Burma. Birbal agreed. Both men set off the very next day with horses, servants and provisions for the trip.

Burma was a long way off, over a thousand miles away. It was a small but independent kingdom, and so far had had little to do with the Mughal emperor.

When Birbal and Hussain Khan finally arrived at the capital of Burma several weeks later, they went straight to the king's palace.

The king of Burma sat on his throne in a splendid palace, surrounded by his ministers and advisors. They were surprised when Akbar's emissaries were ushered in. What could the great emperor possibly want from them?

Hussain Khan's throat felt dry now that the time had come to make his speech. He hastily handed Akbar's letter to Birbal. Without hesitation, Birbal bowed to the king and made a long speech, full of courtly sentiments and lavish compliments. Hussain Khan

couldn't help admiring how quickly Birbal was able to come up with the right things to say, even though he had not had time to prepare.

Birbal handed the sealed scroll over to the king. Both Birbal and Hussain Khan waited eagerly to learn what was in the letter. Birbal usually knew the contents of all the messages he carried for the emperor. This was the first time that he had travelled for so many weeks without knowing what it was.

The king's interpreter repeated the Persian contents of the letter in the Burmese language. Birbal and Hussain Khan could not understand a word he said. But they did notice the effect the letter had on the king and his nobles. They appeared to be utterly shocked and gaped at each other with open mouths.

Akbar's letter had requested that the king of Burma hang the two men who were the bearers of his message, on the night of the full moon. What a strange request! The Burmese peered closely at the two messengers from India. They did not seem to be wicked criminals. The king felt he had to have a meeting with his ministers before deciding what to do with the two strangers from India. Meanwhile, he ordered that the two men be removed from the court and kept under close guard. As soon as they were gone, the nobles clustered around the king.

'Why does Akbar want us to hang these poor fellows? They do not seem to be bad men,' one minister pondered.

'If they did something wrong, why did he not hang them himself?' asked another.

'Perhaps they are powerful men and Akbar is afraid to execute them in his own country,' suggested the chief minister.

'If they are powerful men, then surely it is not safe for us to kill them either. Their friends will come after us.'

'Emperor Akbar is a powerful man too. I cannot ignore this request he has sent all the way to me, or else he will be angry with me,' said the king.

The chief minister had an idea. 'Let me talk to the prisoners and try to learn from them why Emperor Akbar would wish to hang them. Perhaps that will help make things clear.'

Everyone agreed on the plan and the chief minister walked to the room where Birbal and Hussain Khan were kept under guard.

Meanwhile, the two ambassadors were wondering what was going on. Hussain Khan was becoming quite anxious. 'I do not know what was in that letter, Birbal, but it certainly made all of them very unhappy. What is going to become of us?'

'I don't know what will become of us,' said Birbal.

'But it does not look good. The king is treating us like prisoners instead of important guests.'

'I am the emperor's brother-in-law. They should not be treating me like this. I'm counting on you to get us out of this mess, whatever it is, Birbal. You are responsible for my safety. My sister will never forgive you if anyone should harm me.'

'Very well,' said Birbal. 'I will try to get us out of this mess. But you must agree with everything I say. Even repeat what I say, if necessary.'

Just then, the chief minister walked into the room. 'Emperor Akbar has asked us in his letter to hang both of you on the night of the full moon. Can you tell us why he would make such a strange request?'

Hussain Khan went pale and broke out in a sweat, but Birbal replied smoothly. 'But of course. You must follow Emperor Akbar's instructions exactly. Our king is a great and just man. He always has a good reason for everything he does.'

Hussain Khan managed to agree with Birbal as he had promised. 'Yes, yes. You must hang us on the night of the full moon, exactly as Emperor Akbar has ordered.'

The chief minister was even more mystified than before. The two men were actually quite eager to be hanged! And they refused to say why.

He took this information back to the king's council.

'Well, let us go forward with Akbar's instructions,' the king decided.'Perhaps these men will change their minds when they are faced with the gallows, and tell us what this is all about.'

Gallows were constructed in the palace courtyard, and on the night of the full moon, Birbal and Hussain Khan were led to them. The king and his courtiers stood around watching.

In the meanwhile, Birbal had carefully tutored Hussain Khan about what he should say. As planned, Hussain Khan ran forward to the king of Burma.'Your Majesty, I am Emperor Akbar's brother-in-law. I would like to be hanged first.'

'No, no, no!' Birbal protested. 'I was the one who handed you Emperor Akbar's letter, therefore I should be hanged first.'

The king and his ministers were utterly puzzled by this odd behaviour.The chief minister turned to Birbal. 'If you promise to tell us why you are so eager to be hanged, I will make sure you go first.'

'Very well, sire,' said Birbal, pretending to be greatly relieved, while Hussain Khan pouted and appeared to be angry. 'Astrologers have predicted that whoever is hanged first, on this night of the full moon, will become the king of Burma in the next life. Since Hussain Khan and I are closest to Emperor Akbar, he was hoping one of us would be the next king of Burma. This way he can make Burma a part of his empire without fighting a war.'

Aha! So this was Akbar's motive in having these men hanged here on the night of the full moon. No wonder they were eager to be hung first. The king was very concerned. He certainly did not want anyone but his son, the crown prince, to be the next king of Burma. And he never wanted Burma to be a part of Akbar's empire.

He ordered Birbal and Hussain Khan to be set free. The next morning they were carefully escorted out of the borders of the kingdom and sent on their way.

Several weeks later, Birbal and Hussain Khan arrived back at Akbar's court. The emperor greeted them warmly. He had been absolutely sure that Birbal would find a way to escape from the situation he had put them in. Hussain Khan had been taught a frightening lesson.

Akbar turned to his brother-in-law. 'Well, Hussain Khan, do you still wish to take Birbal's place as ambassador and councillor?'

Hussain Khan joined both palms and bowed low. 'Oh no, Your Majesty. Only Birbal can go on these dangerous missions. Only he has the wit and wisdom to handle these situations. I have no desire left to take his place.'

THE

FRIENDSHIP OF

AKBAR AND BIRBAL

The closeness between Akbar and Birbal was enhanced by the fact that the emperor saved his minister's life twice, once at considerable risk to his own safety.

The first time was in 1583, at a polo game that was being played during the celebrations of the Id festival. During the game, Birbal suddenly fell from his horse and became unconscious. It was Akbar who ran to his aid and revived him.

The following year, Akbar and his courtiers were observing an elephant fight at the polo ground. The emperor sat on a horse. In the middle of the fight, an elephant suddenly charged at Birbal. When he saw that his friend was in danger, Akbar urged his horse on and stood between the elephant and Birbal. As the angry elephant rushed at the emperor, the spectators cried out in fear for his life. But Akbar merely commanded the elephant to stop in an imperious manner. Recognizing the voice of authority, the elephant suddenly stopped in its tracks.

Such a close friendship with the great emperor made several people envy Birbal. From many of the stories which have come down to us, it appears that several courtiers were jealous of his closeness to the king and were constantly competing with him.

One such man was the scholar Badauni, who in the second part of his *Muntakhab-ut-Tawarikh* describes Akbar's court. Badauni was fanatical in his religious beliefs, and resented the influence of Abul Fazl and Birbal, who he believed had turned Akbar's mind away from Islam. He was shocked at Birbal for teaching the king strange Hindu ways like worshipping the sun. Badauni called Birbal 'accursed', 'wretch' and 'hellish dog'. He made many negative comments about Birbal's character. He even rejoiced when Birbal was killed in the battle against the Afghans. He blamed the defeat of the Mughal army on Birbal's 'wilfulness and stupidity and arrogance'.

However, Badauni admitted that the emperor 'had never experienced such grief at the death of any Amir' as he did at that of Birbal's. Even though he hated him so much, Badauni described Birbal as being 'possessed of a considerable amount of capacity and genius'. Coming from Badauni, this was high praise indeed.

Like many of Akbar's leading nobles, Birbal was not

only a poet and orator, he was also a brave soldier who eventually commanded an army of 2000 men. He died fighting in February 1586, during a battle against Afghans in Swat, a region on the north-west frontier of India, at the age of fifty-eight.

When the news of Birbal's death reached the emperor, Akbar was devastated. He did not eat for two days and nights. What upset him further was that Birbal's body had not been recovered. He could not even honour him in a state funeral that would show everyone how important he was to him. He missed his favourite companion greatly. It is said that losing Birbal was the greatest grief he had experienced since coming to the throne.

Birbal and the Mad Elephant

Akbar liked taking chances and doing dangerous things. Once, as a young man, he had mounted one of the most violent elephants in the stable and had gone in chase of another elephant. People in the court were aghast because they were sure the emperor would be killed. Instead, Akbar enjoyed the episode very much.

Birbal was a brave man too, but he was far more cautious than his master. 'Why court danger if you can avoid it?' was his belief.

Akbar liked to tease Birbal by putting him in situations where he would have to confront danger. As Birbal had always scolded the king about the dangers of riding violent elephants, Akbar thought he would play a trick on him.

One day, when Birbal was walking towards the palace through a narrow lane, Akbar had one of the most dangerous elephants in the stables let loose. He watched from the balcony to see what Birbal would do. Had Akbar been in his shoes, he probably would have found a way to confront the angry beast and climb on to its back. That is how he did things. He was the king; he had to master every situation.

Birbal believed in using his mind rather than physical power. When he saw the enraged elephant come charging down the narrow lane towards him, he realized he was trapped. If he were to turn around and run back, the elephant would have chased him down and trampled him to death. Suddenly he spotted a stray dog. Swiftly, he lifted up the animal and flung it at the elephant.

Confused by the dog's barks and yelps, the elephant stopped in his tracks. Birbal took advantage of the elephant's hesitation and escaped from the lane.

Akbar clapped his hands. Even though he would have handled the situation differently, he couldn't help admiring Birbal's presence of mind.

The Crows of Agra

Every time the emperor wished to know something, he turned to Birbal. 'Birbal, what . . .?,' 'Birbal, why . . .?,' 'Birbal how . . .?,' he always seemed to be asking, as though Birbal knew everything. This made some of the other nobles at court jealous.

A small group of learned men decided to bring the matter up in court. 'Your Majesty, you consult Birbal for solutions to every problem, as though he is the only man at court with any brains. We are also quite intelligent. Sometimes you should give us the opportunity to serve you.'

'Very well, then,' said the emperor immediately. Some of the scholars at court took themselves so seriously. He loved to poke fun at them. 'Tell me: how many crows are there in the city of Agra?'

The nobles rolled their eyes in astonishment. What

sort of a question was this? Agra was full of crows. Thousands of them. Always cawing and making pests of themselves.

'Surely you jest, Your Majesty. Only Allah would know the answer to this question!' one courtier said, throwing up his hands.

Stroking his beard, another man answered thoughtfully: 'To take a census of the crows, I would need two hundred men or so, Your Majesty. It would take us about a year to get you an accurate count of all the crows in the city.' He saw an opportunity for himself as perhaps the Head of the Bureau of Crow Counting.

'But crows don't sit still to be counted, Your Majesty,' protested a third noble. 'No one can ever claim to get an accurate count of the crows in the city.'

Akbar turned to Birbal who was standing beside him, shielding his smile with his hand. He could see that the king was just having fun at the expense of the discontented nobles. 'Well, Birbal, what do you say? How many crows are there in the city of Agra?'

Without a moment's hesitation, Birbal replied, 'Thirty thousand, four hundred and eighty-three, Your Majesty.'

Immediately, one of the nobles pounced on him. 'It is easy enough to come up with a number. But how do we know it is true? What if we were to actually count the crows and there were less than you say?'

Completely unruffled, Birbal responded quickly. 'Ah, that would only mean that several of the crows of Agra are in other cities visiting their friends and relatives.'

Akbar was thoroughly enjoying the discussion. He loved to see how smoothly Birbal could handle the trickiest of problems.

Unwilling to let go of the argument, the noble persisted. 'But what if there are more crows than thirty thousand, four hundred and eighty-three, Birbal?'

'But of course, they would be the crows from other cities visiting their friends and relatives in Agra.'

Akbar burst out laughing and clapped his hands. Nobody could challenge Birbal's answer. The emperor turned to the downcast nobles. 'Now do you see why I turn to Birbal for everything? He always has the answer.'

Birbal bowed low. But the nobles continued to mutter and grumble about the attention he received from the king.

Long Live the King

Yusuf Khan was envious of Birbal. He seemed so clever and sure of himself. Akbar made it quite obvious that he thought very highly of him. He sent him on important missions and gave him special favours and honours. The emperor seemed to think that Birbal could do no wrong. Wouldn't it be nice if once, just once, Birbal could be made to look foolish in the eyes of the emperor?

Yusuf Khan became quite obsessed with the idea of discrediting Birbal. He waited for a time when Birbal was away from court and then approached Akbar.

'Your Majesty, I have heard Birbal boast that he can read men's minds. No doubt he is a wonderfully clever man. No ordinary human could do such a thing.'

Yusuf Khan's friend, who was part of the scheme, chimed in. 'But everyone knows that Birbal is the cleverest man in the kingdom. Why, reading men's thoughts should be no problem for a genius like him!'

Both men knew that although the emperor loved Birbal, he did get quite irritated when a man other than himself was praised so highly.

And sure enough, Akbar snorted. 'So, Birbal claims he can read men's thoughts, does he? It would be nice then to watch a demonstration of his so-called powers.'

When Birbal returned to court, Yusuf Khan and his friend waited eagerly for the emperor to bring up the subject. At the end of the morning, after Akbar had finished congratulating Birbal on the mission he had just handled so successfully, he commented. 'You are indeed a very clever man, Birbal. I have heard that you claim to be able to read men's minds.'

Birbal had sensed that something was afoot when he had entered the court that morning. Yusuf Khan and his friend were whispering to each other and looking at him in a malicious way. Now, when he glanced in their direction, they were sitting upright, smiling expectantly. He guessed that this was their idea. They were waiting to see him fail in front of the emperor.

Unperturbed, Birbal bowed low. 'Your Majesty honours me too much. How could one as humble and lowly as myself ever read the lofty thoughts of the

King of Kings?'

Then he straightened up and looked around. 'But I can say with confidence that I can read the minds of every one of the men gathered in this room. There is only one thought in all their loyal minds: they pray to the Almighty to bless you with a long and healthy life so that you can rule over us forever.' He turned to Yusuf Khan. 'Well, my dear Yusuf Khan, have I read your mind correctly or do you disagree with me?'

Birbal knew full well that Yusuf Khan would never dare to deny that he was thinking of anything but the king's welfare. None of the nobles in the room had the courage to challenge Birbal's statement. Naturally, they did not wish the king to think they were disloyal. They would have to agree that Birbal had read their minds correctly. One and all murmured their assent. Yusuf Khan squirmed in his chair. Quick-thinking Birbal had avoided the trap that had been so carefully set for him. In fact, he managed to impress Akbar even more with his diplomatic handling of the situation.

Akbar smiled broadly. He realized now what Yusuf Khan had been trying to do and was delighted to see Birbal put him in his place.

Birbal Goes to Heaven

Some courtiers could not get over their hatred for Birbal. They blamed their lack of success in court not on their abilities, but on Birbal. If Birbal were not around, perhaps they would get promoted.

A few of them hated him so passionately that they plotted to kill him. They took Akbar's barber into their confidence. Since he shaved the king every day, he had an opportunity to speak privately to the king without Birbal around. They gave the barber a bag of gold coins and promised him more if their plot succeeded. The greedy barber thought this was an easy way to make some money.

The next day when he was shaving Akbar, he said, 'Your Majesty, have you ever thought of what life must be like in the next world? For example, wouldn't it be nice to know how your father, His Majesty, Emperor

Humayun, God rest his soul, is doing in the other world? I often wonder if he is happy and if he needs anything.'

'Yes, it would be nice to know,' Akbar admitted. 'But I have no means of finding out.'

'Perhaps I can help you here, Your Majesty,' the barber suggested eagerly. 'I recently met a holy man who can send people to the other world . . .'

'Hah! That is easy enough to do!' the emperor snorted. 'All I have to do is to execute someone to send him to the other world.'

'But this holy man gave me a mantra that can bring them back, sire!' the barber exclaimed. 'I saw with my own eyes. He piled a thousand bales of hay on an open field. Then he burned a man alive on this huge pyre. All the man had to do was to chant the mantra just before the fire was lit. Later, the man returned from the other world and told everyone how he had met his departed relatives there.'

'It sounds perfectly simple, but whom should we send? Would you like to go?' offered the emperor, wondering where this strange story would lead to.

'Oh no, not me!' the barber replied immediately, breaking out into a sweat. 'I am not important enough to go to heaven, sire. Your ancestors would be most insulted if a most humble and miserable speck of dust like myself were to inquire after them! It should be someone really important, Your Majesty. Someone you trust completely. Someone wise and clever who can conduct himself in any situation. For example, a man such as Raja Birbal. A perfect choice!'

'Aha!' thought Akbar, when he heard Birbal's name. 'So this is yet another plot to get rid of Birbal. Let me play along with this foolish man and see what happens. Birbal will teach him a lesson.' He was completely confident that Birbal would find a way out of the predicament. He always did.

At court that day, the emperor summoned Birbal and informed him that he had decided to send him as an ambassador to heaven to inquire after his dead father's health and comfort. The wicked nobles who had plotted Birbal's downfall rubbed their hands in glee to see their plans succeeding.

'It will be my greatest honour, Jahanpanah! My life and everything I own are at your disposal,' said Birbal bowing low. He immediately realized that this was the work of his enemies. He knew he had lots of them at court. 'But please, Your Majesty, may I have a month to prepare for this journey? Who knows if and when I will return?'

'Gladly!' said the emperor. 'You may have as much time as you want.'

Birbal hired some trusted workmen to build a secret

tunnel from the open field outside the city to his home. When it was ready, he had a thousand bundles of hay piled right next to the hidden opening of the secret tunnel.

On the appointed day, Akbar, his nobles, indeed the entire town turned out to see Birbal embark on this strange journey to heaven. Birbal sat atop the bundles of hay and chanted the mantra that the barber had given him. Then, saluting the emperor, he gave the order to light the pyre. Amid the flames, smoke, noise and confusion, Birbal escaped through the door of the secret tunnel.

Birbal remained in hiding for several months. The wicked nobles were delighted. It seemed that at long last they had succeeded in getting rid of Akbar's favourite.

Akbar, meanwhile, was getting sadder and sadder without Birbal's cheerful company. Surely, Birbal had found a way to escape from the fire. But where on earth was he?

Then one day, Birbal reappeared at court. No one recognized him. His hair was shaggy and unkempt, and he had grown a long beard. He bowed low at Akbar's feet. Of course, Akbar was overjoyed to see him again.

'Jahanpanah, I am back from heaven. I met His Majesty, the Emperor Humayun, your dear departed father, God rest his soul, and he sends you his love.'

'Well, how is my dear father?' said Akbar, playing along with Birbal for the benefit of the court. The wicked nobles sat astounded to see their rival, safe and sound, returned from the dead.

'He is very happy and contented,' said Birbal. 'Except for one thing. There are no barbers in heaven. You see how shaggy and unkempt my hair has become in just a few weeks ...You can imagine what your father looks like!'

'I know just the man to do the job,' Akbar chuckled delightedly. Birbal had found the perfect way to pay back his enemies. He summoned the greedy barber to the court and informed him that he was sending him to heaven to cut his father's hair.

'Prepare to ascend the pyre tomorrow,' he ordered.

The barber took to his heels and was never seen again!

Bibliography

Abul Fazl. *Akbarnama*, trans. by H. Beveridge, Delhi, 1989
—— *Ain-i-Akbari*, trans. by H. Blochmann et al., Delhi, 1977
Amar Chitra Katha. *Tales of Birbal*
—— *More Tales of Birbal*
Badauni, Abd al-Qadir. *Muntakhab al-Tavarikh*, trans. Ranking, Lowe & Haig, Delhi, 1973
Beach, Milo C. *The Imperial Image: Paintings for the Mughal Court*, Washington DC, 1981
Brand, Michael & Glenn D. Lowry (ed). *Fatehpur-Sikri: A Sourcebook*, Cambridge MA, 1985
—— *Akbar's India: Art from the Mughal City of Victory*, New York, 1985
Gascoigne, Bamber. *The Great Moghuls*, New York, 1971
Misra, Rekha. *Women in Mughal India* (1526–1748 AD), Delhi, 1967
Moosvi, Shireen. *Episodes in the Life of Akbar: Contemporary Records and Reminiscences*, New Delhi, 1994
Mukundan, Monisha. *Akbar and Birbal: Tales of Humour*, Calcutta, 1992

Naim, C.M. 'Popular Jokes and Political History: The Case of Akbar, Birbal and Mulla Do-Piyaza,' *Economic and Political Weekly*, 17 June 1995

Ramanajun, A.K. *Folktales from India*, New York, 1991

Richards, John F. 'The Formulation of Imperial Authority under Akbar and Jahangir' in *Kingship and Authority in South Asia*, edited by John F. Richards, University of Wisconsin, 1978

Rizvi, Saiyid Athar Abbas. *Religious and Intellectual History of the Muslims in Akbar's Reign (with special reference to Abu'l Fazl)*, Delhi, 1975

Sinha, Parmeshwar Prasad. *Raja Birbal Life and Times*, Patna, 1980

Thapar, Romila. *Indian Tales*, Delhi, 1991

Thomas, Vernon. *Tales of Birbal and Akbar*, New Delhi, 1982

OTHER BOOKS IN THE SERIES:

Vikram and Vetal
Stories of Tenali Raman